# Pomfret

## Short Stories

## Edited by Brian Lewis

I0547756

## Nettle Books
## in association with
## Pontefract Press

Supported using public funding by

ARTS COUNCIL
ENGLAND

Pomfret

First published by Nettle Books
www.nettlebooks.weebly.com

in association with Pontefract Press
brian@pontefractpress.co.uk

Second edition published by Nettle Books
nettlebooks@hotmail.co.uk


Classification: Fiction
ISBN: 978-0-9561513-8-4

Cover design: Wayne Clarida
Cover picture: Reini Schuhle


Events and characters in these stories are imaginary or historical. Any similarity to living persons is coincidental.

Opinions expressed are not necessarily those of the authors, editors or publishers.


© Copyright of the stories remains with the individual authors. All rights reserved.

© Copyright of the illustrations remains with the individual artists. All rights reserved.

# Introduction

You take a town – in this case Pontefract in Yorkshire – and an age group and a unifying theme.

You set a very tight publication deadline and find a local printer. It is agreed that the form is a short story about 2000 words long and you print the invitations to the book launch. You let it be known that you are in business by talking to local people and canvassing local reader and writer groups.

I have been editor, last-minute illustrator and general Go-for. Michael Yates has been involved in proof reads and is our protector against typographical improprieties.

We call our group 'The Bus Pass People' because you have to be 60+ to be involved. Finally, we are grateful to Arts Council England and the Lottery Fund for providing us with a grant for the project.

Brian Lewis, March 2016

# Contents

Second Soprano ...................................................5

Crossroads of the North ...................................13

Fowl Business in Suburbia ..............................22

The Place of the Badgers................................28

Princess Annabel's Birthday Party.................34

The Museum Rocking Horse............................40

James Edward Smith ......................................47

Mrs T and the Buffaloes .................................51

Liquorice Faire .................................................60

If Only They'd Known ......................................71

# Second Soprano

*Michael Yates*

*Artist: Brian Lewis*

CLEM SUMMERS suspected he was already dead when he started re-reading *Sherlock Holmes*.

He started with the novels. *A Study in Scarlet* held good memories for him and he still enjoyed Watson's list of Sherlock's skills and knowledge, especially: *Knowledge of Literature – Nil, Knowledge of Sensational Literature – Immense*. But when he got to *The Hound of the Baskervilles*, he was appalled by the silliness and the amount of padding. He decided not to bother with the five volumes of short stories, though he'd already uploaded two replacement copies to his Kindle at a cost of 99p each.

It was no better when he came to old movies in his DVD collection. He started with Hitchcock and *North by Northwest,* still pretty good. But the scenery in *The Thirty-Nine Steps* was obviously a painted backdrop and the Alpine hotel of *The Lady Vanishes* was a table-top model, and this irked him. He'd intended to play his old Dylans and Rolling Stones a lot, but had recently settled for a CD of Mozart's *Requiem.*

The choir he'd joined last year – Pomfret Polyphonic – were planning to perform it for their September concert at St Giles's near the Buttercross, and he needed to learn the bass parts.

He tried to explain it to Audrey: how the books, music and films were monuments. Over the years, he had kept up his libraries, filled his shelves, not so much with the intention of reading or listening or viewing the things again; but because they were part of his life and he could always glance at them and know exactly who Clem Summers was. But now he'd got to 63 and retired from the insurance business, they seemed more like millstones than milestones. Now he said: "I don't love them any more. I don't love *me* any more." What he meant was: he didn't love *her* any more.

Every Tuesday morning she sat in the padded green armchair in the Carleton Haven care home, her head propped against a pillow, her chin dropped down on her chest, her face turned away. One time, Care Assistant Jackie had plumped up her pillow and moved her head so she was looking directly at him. Jackie said: "There, Mrs Summers, isn't your husband a fine figure of a man?"

And Audrey said: "He promised to come. He promised to visit. But he never does." To Audrey he was already dead.

The choir came together every Tuesday evening in a narrow street off Beastfair, in rehearsal rooms which had once been a Poundshop and now had an upright piano and an electric kettle. Clem hummed the *Dies Irae* as he parked his Ford Focus in Tesco's car park. When he got out, he noticed the woman locking her Renault near the bottle bank was looking at him intently. She was maybe his own age: slim, freckled, dyed red hair, *still a fine figure* as Jackie would say. The woman said: "It's Clem Winter, isn't it?"

"Summers," he corrected her.

"Summers. Sorry. You probably don't remember. You sold life insurance to my husband Harold."

A moment of panic gripped Clem. His recurring nightmare was being approached by an angry client whose loved one had died outside the clauses and conditions of some policy he'd sold.

"I hope Harold's well," he said.

"He's been dead two years."

"I hope..." He was embarrassed and could not complete the sentence.

But she caught on right away. "Oh, the money was fine. I mean, I paid off the mortgage OK." She smiled. She had beautiful teeth.

Now they were both embarrassed. He'd forced her to sound cheerful about her husband's death.

She said: "It's just that I went to school with Audrey.

7

That's why we came to you in the first place. Give her my love, will you? It's Erica Stoppard. Used to be Erica Dickens. How is she these days?"

He didn't want to say *head propped on pillow, chin dropped down on chest*. He said: "She's fine. I'll remember you to her." And he might, though it would make no difference.

They walked towards the rehearsal rooms. He said: "You're in the choir too?" Now he felt bad he'd not recognised her. But there *were* 48 people...

"I joined two weeks ago. Second soprano."

They went in to the singing.

There was always a moment when Jackie would say: "You'll want to have a chat, memories, private things. So I'll leave you." And she went off, making a big noisy thing of closing the door, and was gone for 40 minutes exactly. Clem used the time to think about the rest of his day: what he'd get in for supper, what he'd got recorded from Freeview to fill the later part of the evening, phoning Audrey's sister Thelma in Devon to give the weekly report. Maybe a bottle of wine...

He always chose 12 per cent Chardonnay, £7 in Tesco; and was picking it off the shelf, when a voice said: "You and Audrey celebrating tonight?"

It was Erica Stoppard. It took him a moment to understand what she'd said. Then he straightened up, put the bottle in his basket. He said: "Well..." Well what? He still couldn't say: *Head propped on pillow.* "The truth is we're not together these days."

"You're not divorced?"

"No, no. I misled you. I said she was fine. She's not really fine at all."

"Oh no!" Erica put a hand to her mouth. "How long ago?"

"It's 18 months now."

"She's passed away! And you let me go on about Harold! I'm so sorry."

"Yes. Passed away." It was no more than the truth.

She touched his arm. "I know how you feel. With me, it was Tia Maria. And waking up in front of the telly next morning."

Clem said: "Chardonnay is cheaper." And they both laughed.

After a while she said: "Well, got to get on." And she touched his arm again and was gone.

Next time he was with Audrey and Jackie was out of the room, he spent the time thinking about Erica. He thought about the touch on the arm. *Two* touches. Maybe he should… what? Ask her round for a meal? Offer to cook something? At what point would he have to say for the second time: "No, no, I misled you"? It didn't bear thinking about.

"I could cook something," said Erica, "It would make a change." It was during what he always thought of as the bottled water break. The *Lacrimosa* had not gone well and Nathan the musical director had lambasted the sopranos for not looking at him.

"Heads high!" he'd shouted, "Hold the music high!" Afterwards Nathan had a quiet chat with Erica and she'd come out of it looking crestfallen.

When she asked Clem what he thought of the sopranos, he'd said: "Very nice."

And she'd said: "No, it's *you* that's being nice." And she told him how she'd joined the choir because it was only a ten-minute drive from the flat she'd bought in Ackworth. Since her daughter Simone had gone to live in Australia with her boyfriend, there was no need for a big house any more.

Clem told her he and Audrey didn't have children, letting her think it was a conscious decision so he wouldn't have to mention the long-ago miscarriage and complications.

9

That was when Erica invited him to the flat. He heard himself say: "Yes, that would be nice."

On the Saturday night they ate Avocado Vinaigrette, Loin of Pork Dijonnaise and Pavlova ("It's all out of Delia," said Erica) and she kissed him and they went to bed. He'd brought a bottle of wine. "Well," she said, "if you've gone to all the expense of Asti Spumante, you'll want your money's worth."

And he felt he'd come alive again. A little bit.

They started a routine: cinema on Wednesdays (Erica liked Judi Dench); a meal out on Fridays (Italian or Chinese); and Saturdays of TV, CDs (humming along with bits from the Mozart), then Erica's cooking, and finally bed, always at *her* place. He was back home after Sunday breakfast, knowing that Erica had her own activities the rest of the day. He must ask her some time what she did with her Sundays.

The next time he saw Audrey and Jackie did the noisy thing with the door, he said: "I've got something to tell you." Audrey made no move. No show of hearing. No show of listening.

"I don't know how to say it." But he *did* know how to say it; he'd been rehearsing it as often as the *Dies Irae*. "I'm seeing somebody." It sounded ridiculous, a phrase like that from a man of his age. Seeing! What on earth did it mean? "It's somebody you know. Erica Stoppard." Then: "Erica Dickens." Adding lamely: "You were at school together."

Audrey turned swiftly, gripped his wrist tightly, pushed her face against his and said: "She always was a bitch." And then she died. Oh, it could have been a fainting fit. But no, he knew she was dead. In that instant. He leapt to his feet and called out for Jackie.

Clem realised Audrey had forced a crisis in his recently well-ordered life. He now had to tell Erica the truth. It was beyond him to organise the vicar and the undertakers, invite Thelma and Audrey's nephews and her friends from the Women's Walking group, and not mention it to Erica. There was also the guilt thing. He'd *killed* Audrey. There was no other way of looking at it. He'd said the one thing that had the power to penetrate her mind and the shock had finished her.

But to tell Erica the truth – even if he left out that final cruel detail – would be to acknowledge the earlier lie. He steeled himself. He went to the Malt Shovel and had two double whiskies. Then he went home, sobered up with coffee and a nap. Finally he drove round to her flat. It was Tuesday anyway and he would be seeing her in an hour; but this was something he couldn't just slip into the usual five minutes of bottled water time.

She was surprised to see him. Clem said: "People tell lies."

"Do they?"

"And they always get found out. It's never any good." He took a deep breath.

"No, I suppose not," said Erica. She also took a deep breath. "There was no way I could tell you about Nathan. It wasn't just you. It would mean letting the whole choir find out. It was... well, you know he's married. He can only get out once a week."

"You mean Sundays."

In *The Case of the Dubious Philatelist*, Dr Watson had sustained a blow to the back of the neck and "the room had swum like a turbulent sea". Now Clem knew what that meant. He ran out of the flat, down the stairs, scrambled into the Ford and drove...

And he was suddenly in the centre of town. He imagined Nathan waiting in the rehearsal rooms, even now fingering the upright piano, laying his baton on the music stand, dreaming of another Sunday. Clem turned his Ford too fiercely into

Tesco's Car Park and hit the bottle bank.

KEEEEE-RANNNNGGGGGG!!!

The force of the crash hurled him out of his seat, banged his head against the dashboard, but the seat belt (which he couldn't remember remembering) pulled him back again. He clawed frantically at the belt buckle, lurched against the door so hard the pain surged through his shoulder, pulled himself out into fresh air, staggered. He looked at his hands; they were shaking. He looked at his knees; they trembled.

People were leaping out as they parked their cars. It was the choir. *En masse*, they rushed towards him, touched him, held him, steadied him, spoke in words he couldn't immediately grasp but in a tone he understood.

He was alright, they said. He was alive.

*Alive! Yes, he was!*

And he laughed. And the choir, surprised, laughed too – sopranos and altos, tenor and bass. And it built to a crescendo.

It was the first time he'd heard them in proper harmony.

# Crossroads of the North

*John A Goodrich*

*Artist: Jane Walsh*

IT WAS 1935, a normal night shift on the Swinton and Knottingley Joint Railway.

The stove had to be stoked up again, that lazy devil always runs it low for the end of his shift at Ten. One of these mornings, when I finish at Six, I'll let the bugger die right out and see how he likes that, cheeky little sod. As I told our lass: "Marge," I said, "If our Mary marries him, she'll have to do the bloody lot herself."

"Much like me then, Henry." She says, cheeky sod. She does all right, she does.

I turned out to be wrong though: Jim did marry my Mary and it seems that at home he ain't so lazy as he is at work Not *idle*, you understand, we can't be idle in the box. No, not idle, just bloody lazy. He went to Germany, you know, just last year, he cracked a good'un when he got back, he'd been in a box over there, he said the German for signalman is *Dasleverpuschenpullenmister.* I thought that was a bloody good mouthful.

10.30: Ah, here's the up Birmingham train, he's through the junction in good time today. I gave the old 1-2-2 bell code to Baghill box down the line; his semaphores are always green for the two fish trains. Bit of time to spare now for stoking up and a little read if the lamps hold out.

*A poor Ferrybridge woman was robbed of her rent money on Fishergate as she made her way home from the market. She shouted after the robber that the cash was for her rent. Two hours later her cottage had an open window and someone threw in a leather bag containing gold and silver to the sum of six pounds. John Palmer had robbed her but took pity and returned her money fivefold.*

See, it's true what they say, John Palmer cared for poor people. I told my Marge about this, she shrugged her shoulders. "I never heard about that, was it last week then, Henry?"

"No," I says, "It was in April 1736. John Palmer was the real name of the famous highwayman Dick Turpin. But it happened in Ferrybridge though, Marge."

"Well, my Grandad always did say: Crossroads of the North, that's Ferrybridge."

12.15am: 1-2-2 code    rang. Here's the down Woodford fitted goods. I'll just get him through my section, then I'll get back to some serious study for about half an hour. It's amazing what one can learn at work, ain't it? I'd better not let our Jim know or he'll be doing some serious negligence, not that he's much of a student of history, him. Still, the job provides for our Mary so I suppose he's all right really. I hope he don't batter her about like his dad battered his mother. Ended up in the Almshouses, she did, you know, up the street facing Mayfield Terrace.

If that had been my own old man, I'd have swung for him. No, he suffered enough though, *my* Dad did, he was in the thick of it over in Belgium in 1917. They never want to talk about it though, do they?

Talking of the Almshouses, my Uncle Tommy used to say that it was wide enough to turn a coach and four around between Mayfield Terrace and  the Almshouses. One day, back in the late 1800s, a coachman *did* swing his coach and four around but it all ended sadly. The coach wheels hit a pothole. If there was a piece of road on a good bit of clay, it was often dug up a bit, and the clay was used to make pots which were used for bottle moulds at the glassworks, that's where *pot-holes* come from, everybody knows that.

Any road up, one of the frightened passengers was thrown out of the coach door as it spun round, and she landed in an indecorous heap right up against the door of the Almshouses, and laid there with her frilly bloomers for all to see. Only a dozen or so actually witnessed it, but it was hot news in the Greyhound and the Lion by evening time.

She was Lady Hermione Victoria Fox-Brotherton, from down south somewhere. Now she was notorious in Ferrybridge, Crossroads of the North.

The Almshouses were still a hospital in those days so they only had to move her six feet to get her into a bed. Her health and shoulder injury was restored in no time, but her dignity took a while to restore.

It had been the first public showing of frilly bloomers ever seen in the town, and she was a lady too. She was never seen again after that. She was remembered though, or so my uncle told us. Them Almshouse rooms have seen some sights, but they've seen illness and suffering too over the years.

Back in the box. Only a few down trains now before the next up train at 3.05, just respond to Jack at Baghill box and just pull off my section signals three or four times. I can do that in my sleep, but actually of course I'm fully alert because I'm having a little read, the railway is completely safe in my hands. Yes, Crossroads of the North is under expert control. Ahem, I hope there's no specials tonight that'll throw me. Haha! Did you know my station nameboards say 'Ferrybridge-for-Knottingley?' Not many people know that, but they do, we're important you know. Now, where's my book?

What's this? Aha, War of the Roses.

*The War of the Roses led to events at Ferrybridge, it being the most convenient river crossing for the eighteen-year-old King Edward IV who marched his Yorkist army from London to the north prior to the battle of Towton in March 1461. On his arriving in Ferrybridge in late March however, the River Aire bridge had been damaged by retreating Lancastrian Red Rose forces, and repairs were needed. The bridge keepers, ordinary Ferrybridge folk, had been brutally murdered and the townspeople were, as they say, 'up in arms,' or they would have been if the King had let them. Edward's Yorkist army set to work to repair the bridge and a stand-off*

16

*ensued as some 500 Lancastrians led by Clifford were on the north side of the bridge.*

*This was likely to hold things up a bit, so King Edward despatched some men under one of his leaders, Fauconberg, to Castleford three miles away, to cross the Aire via the ancient Roman ford in that town. Lancastrian defenders of the ford were not yet in place and Fauconberg was able to cross at the ford and march back to Ferrybridge.*

*He rejoined King Edward and assisted by attacking the Red Rose forces on their flank. The Lancastrians had no heart for this battle, and took flight northwards. They were pursued and were caught at Dinting Dale, a shallow depression across the Tadcaster road near Barkston. Here, almost in sight of the Lancastrian forces, they were killed.*

*Fauconberg and Edward's army then withdrew a few miles and camped at the settlement of Sherburn. The Battle of Towton Moor took place on the following day. Palm Sunday 29<sup>th</sup> March 1461*

See, what have I told you! Crossroads of the north it is round here. Even William Shakespeare wrote about it. Oh by the way, all that puts me in mind of Fanny Dark, she was a beauty in her younger days. Round about 1912, Fanny got herself 'up the duff.' Well, actually Sammy Albright got her up the duff.

Now Fanny was a beauty, a handsome girl she was. Oh aye, I've said that once already. No, she was big up top, you know. It was that that attracted Sammy. Fair smitten he was. She said he brought Light into her Dark. Well, Fanny had a fearsome reputation for a temper, a real bossy britches she was. Of course, when Sammy got her up the duff, it was her that told him that they were going to get married. He had no choice didn't Sammy, except join the Navy or something, and he wouldn't do that because he couldn't swim, and anyway he had a great job. They were earning fifty bob a week in 1913. He was a glass blower up Bagley's at

17

Knottingley. Sammy was a craftsman. Mind you, it was easy for him 'cos he was always full of wind, was Sammy. We nicknamed the pair of 'em Gusty and Busty.

Any road up, when she told him they were going to marry, he insisted on Palm Sunday, because he said it would be a bloodbath, and the Battle of Towton, bloodiest battle ever, was fought on Palm Sunday. Now I knew Fanny Albright better in her later days, she was big below as well as up top when I knew her, broad in front and broad behind, she was. When all the women stood in their doorways talking or shouting at each other as they did in those days, Fanny filled her doorway right up, you couldn't get a fag paper between her and the door frame. Sammy was indeed a light unto her. They had nine kids, so it was Albright everywhere.

Sammy retired from the glass works and helped out at the canal lock in town. He also spent hours and hours in the little marsh or main marsh between Ferry' and Brotherton. This was a natural flood plain. There are many named marshes round here and along to marsh end in Knottingly near the boat builders.

In fact, the road up to Brotherton is called Marsh Bridge, part of the old Great North Road it is. The road there was raised up on masonry about four or five feet above the level of the marsh. Gusty Albright used to do his bird-watching in that area. But then, one winter day this year, he was on the pony bridge at the lock, he slipped on ice and fell in. He drowned there and then. Gusty was gone.

Right. I've got those down trains through to York, just a couple more of them, then three up trains, and my shift will be over. It's a bugger is nights. I come to the box when everyone is down at the Lion, and I go home before anybody gets up in the morning, except a couple of friends who work at Fryston pit, they usually walk to work, just a couple of miles. Mind you, I wouldn't relish walking home after a shift in the pit, would you?

"Doughty," they always say, "It's a doddle for you, sat there in a nice warm signal box."

They don't know the responsibility I have. It was a right busy job before the 1914 war, they tell me, but if owt, I think it's even busier now. Got a couple of days off now though, so I'll get a few pints of Darley's mild down me, I'll tell them miners just how hard it is in my box. One time, I used to watch Bob Carter, the local carter; he had a couple of wagons in the early days but he soon got on, then he bought a large delivery van. He delivered all over the East Riding, as far as Beverley and Hull. I seen him more than once when he picked up a schoolteacher from the school, I could see from my box. I thought nothing of it till much later. Then one warm summer night, it was still light and I was standing outside the box having a Woodbine, when to my surprise Bob's wife walked along the platform right up to the box.

"Here," I said "You can't come up here, Betty, it's against the rules. What are you doing?"

"Bugger the rules, Henry, I want to ask you a few questions." I was all ears.

"Have you seen my Bob in the goods yard delivering stuff to the goods office?"

"Course I have, you're always in the van as well aren't you?" (I slipped up there.)

"I never go in his bloody van, but you've told me what I needed. Thanks, Henry."

"Well Betty, the office is over the yard, I couldn't see very clearly. Sorry."

"Don't worry, Henry. I know it's that Facility... er, Felicity, that bloody teacher. You know my old man has been doing well lately, he's been dabbling on the stock exchange. He's made a bit in shares and that. I know what he's doing with her. He's exercising his options in the horizontal plane, the dirty bugger. I'll have that Facility. . . er. . . Felicity, she'll need a facility when I've done with her. The tramp. Thanks,

Henry." She left the box. I had to laugh, yet I felt for her. Old Bob eh? What a turn up, all the world is here

I thought: Wait till I get in the Greyhound, I'll enjoy that Darley's again for sure!

Forty years later: Jack Doughty, 15 years old in 1976, put down the notebooks that had entertained him throughout the summer holidays. Jack had not taken a strong interest in local history or any history really, but his Grandad's scribblings had gripped him since he'd found the old diary and journal in the garden shed at Grandma Marge's house on the Wentcliff side of town.

He had a favourite spot up there. He could see the brand spanking new motorway which passed almost through his own front yard. Two broad and clean and gleaming three-lane carriageways carrying so little traffic. East to Hull and the docks, and West to Leeds and Manchester. Hull in under an hour, Manchester in not much over an hour. Marvellous! *Ferrybridge, the Crossroads of the North,* he thought. But, come to think about it, actually, it all but bypassed Ferrybridge.

Yet there was the A1 north to south, the railway in any direction you want. M62 east or west, the canal still active and carrying oil tankers. The canal also had floating coal trains of 'Tom Puddings,' 30 of them, pulled by a tug. Each Tom Pudding held thirty-five tons of coal or more, heading for docks at Hull either for distribution at home or abroad. Grain was carried on the canal to Castleford Allinsons mill or further on to Leeds, coal for everywhere. Cars screaming by every-which-way, day and night on the Motorways. Bloody marvellous. Grandad and the old blokes were right.

Those cyclists and ramblers and such just pass through here nowadays, they know nothing of our glorious past. Crossroads of the North. My home, Ferrybridge. The town people are as friendly and as kind as ever, we nestle beneath all the action a bit these days, quiet Town Street, Fishergate, Pollards, the refinery, glassworks and all that are just down the road, plenty of work. We generate power from 'A' 'B' and 'C' power stations for the whole of Britain. Yes, it's great here.

"Grandma Marge!"

"Yes, lad?" she answered.

"Grandad Henry's old books and stuff are great. Fancy writing all that at work!"

"It was only thought up in that box, love. It was written in that shed where he hid himself away so as he wouldn't have to go up the allotment. Your grandad Henry and the two Henry Doughtys before him, they were the same, left the digging to us women. He was right as usual though, Crossroads of the North and all that stuff."

"Yeah, it's a good read, Grandma."

"Bet he didn't write about that Betty Carter breaking rule 72, did he? He thought I didn't know about that, rule 72 says no unauthorised person is allowed in any signal box and Betty Carter was certainly unauthorised, I can tell you. But I know she was in there one night, not to mention a couple of tramps sometimes in the winter."

Jim laughed quietly to himself and smiled, but then he said: "He did put it all down, Grandma. I've read it, it was quite innocent, honest."

She smoothed her pinny down, "Oh, right. Well, I shall have to have a look then. Want some tea, love? I'm brewing up."

# Fowl Business in Suburbia

*Howard Frost*

*Artist: Barbara Smith*

I WAS IN Pontefract for a meeting the other day as I very occasionally am, when who should I meet as I strolled down Horsefair to catch a bus back to where I'd left the car but my old junior school chum Juddy!

We had been chums almost by default, being two new boys at the beginning of the Easter Term in a very snowy January. My family and I were living with my maternal grandmother for three months in Cridling Stubbs, one of the small villages near Ponte whilst our house in the town was ready; and Juddy had just moved in with his family to a house across the street from my grandmother's house, as his father had been moved to Kellington, one of the National Coal Board collieries.

George – or Juddy, or Judda, he answered to all three and I never knew what his surname was – travelled back home for lunch, as I did. And, since we were both in the same class and as there was a convenient bus each way, we used it and saved the mile and a half walk.

Now Juddy had arrived from a junior school in Sharlston, another mining village about 15 miles away where the Yorkshire accent was even more pronounced than that used in my grandmother's village. So he taught me his version in course of our daily non-classroom conversation, which came in handy as a barrier against bullying for being "foreign".

Juddy was one of those "different" boys who, like myself, were neither good at, nor interested in, football, rugby, or even cricket. I enjoyed "backyard cricket", played by six or eight boys where one was certain to get a go at bowling, or with the bat; but the interminable eleven-a-side games at school – out in the blazing sun at deep-fine-leg where the chances of a ball coming anywhere near one were slim – were boring. I liked reading, Juddy liked "farls" as he called them i.e. fowls, or chickens.

Juddy went all over Yorkshire, mainly on the back of

his father's motorbike, to visit shows where there were classes for hens. He wasn't interested in "fancy poultry" with fluffy legs or even fluffier heads, not he. He was building a picture of the perfect allotment hen and the perfect method of husbandry to produce the maximum number of eggs per bird and the ideal weight of carcase for "killing out", as he put it.

I got to know Juddy's previous school quite well later on when I had to visit it regularly for one of the jobs I did. The head teacher Mr Parkin was also nuts about hens and had an extensive "Balfour System" poultry "farm" for want of a more appropriate word, right next to the school, which was run and managed by a co-operative of nine- and ten-year-old schoolchildren under his supervision.

"You see, Nicholas," he said to me, "it's a wonderful classroom tool. My teachers and I use it to teach weights and measures, and of course simple book keeping and accounts. It adds to the school's income, which goes both towards items for the school like books and items for the children themselves, such as trips and holidays. Not only this, but it provides some children, particularly those who move away, with the means to create a potential income."

So, when I saw my friend Juddy again after a long period during which I had not seen him running his egg stall on Ponte outdoor market, my opening gambit was: "Nar then, Juddy, har yor an har's t'farls?" (Translation: "Hello George, how are you keeping, and how are your chickens?")

Juddy's reply momentarily threw me. He said "It's buggered, an' I've getten no cock nar what wi' yon' bloody council. Let's go hev a cuppa and ar'll tell thi all abart it."

When I had cleared my head of the image of violent physical retribution taken on my friend's manhood by a set of enraged councillors, I began to grasp the truth of the matter, that my friend had been deprived of his cockerel – and that, in consequence, his egg and poultry business was ruined.

Juddy took me to a quiet little café he knew in Gillygate, and when we'd sat down and been provided with some tea, I said "Har's that?" meaning "Why, wherefore and for what reason?"

For the sake of clarity, I'll give you the bare bones of the matter. Juddy said he kept a total flock of approximately 30 birds whose laying he regulated in winter, firstly by the use of artificial light whilst confining a few in their hut; secondly by having cleverly bred a totally new breed of "super hen", which produced eggs for a longer period of the year than virtually every other breed he'd been able to find in his many years of researching the subject; and thirdly by constantly hatching chicks to add to the flock and culling the older birds to sell for meat.

I chipped in to tell him Mr Parkin would have been proud of him.

"He is – well proud!" said Juddy, "tha knaws he come ter work wi' mi after he retired?"

I was not aware that Mr Parkin and Juddy had ever been in business together, and said so. "But what about the Council?" I asked, "Where do they fit into all this, and what have they to do with your cockerel?"

Juddy asked if I remembered where his hens "lived", and I said of course I did because it was next to his grandfather's allotment on the big patch of allotments nearly behind my grandmother's house. I reminded Juddy that I had in fact helped him and his father when they started to erect the first shed and outside fencing. My friend said it had all been replaced and renewed several times since then and, of course, it had grown.

Then came an era of change and the Council had sold half the allotment land off for the building of about 50 private "Yuppie Sheds" as Juddy rather amusingly called them. He said I wouldn't know the old area any longer – no collieries, nature reserves where the old colliery waste tips had been, a big "Glasshoughton shopping mole" as he called it, no railways or canal and lots of "posh frock" type jobs. I retorted that I knew things were changing and I hadn't quite lost touch with my other relatives throughout the area.

"Ar – but fowk has changed" said Juddy and I asked what he meant and *how* had they changed.

"Well," he said – and here I'll translate and cut out the swearing!

He referred to our childhood and how numerous people had kept hens and rabbits for the table and one man we knew kept a pig – allegedly in his front room. Where there were hens, Juddy said, there had to be the occasional cockerel, because nature couldn't run its course otherwise; and years ago, people were more tolerant of cocks crowing at dawn and miners going down the streets wearing hobnailed boots or clogs at 5 am to go on the dayshift at six in the morning. There were few televisions and dawn to dusk was the length of many working people's day.

The owners of the new houses, however, were much less tolerant of Juddy's feathered boss man and his sunrise love calls. He had tried to explain, but to no avail; indeed he had lost two expensive creatures to killers who had tried to emulate the methods of a fox in order to fool him about the real killers. Juddy had laid low with an old shotgun he had – quite legally for anti-vermin purposes – and loosed it off when he heard a noise. Following this, he said, he had a visit from the village bobby.

"Is it still our old chum 'Donkey'?" I asked. Juddy replied that of course it wasn't, as Donkey would have been over 100 years old by now; but funnily enough it was Donkey's son 'Arry'.

Apparently there had been a 'sharp exchange of views' on the subject of whether the occupants of the new houses were vermin or not and Juddy had laid Arry low with a well-timed uppercut. Fortunately Arry had chosen not to arrest him, but the Council were not so lenient about the affair when the complaints about the cock crowing and shotgun firing reached their ears – and Juddy had been told in no uncertain terms that their pest control officer had been ordered to confiscate Juddy's cockerel. Juddy had been to the Council Offices to explain the vital part in his replacement breeding scheme played by young, fit, amorous cockerels with loud voices, and they had more or less said they didn't want to know; and in fact they had much rather he did not run his poultry business where it was and why didn't he go out into the countryside if he wanted to run a farming business?

"So there we are," he said, "I'm ruined by the advance of t' new housing."

"You might almost say it was Fowl business in Suburbia," I said.

And so it is.

# The Place of the Badgers

*Colin Hollis*

**Artist: Colin Hollis**

HE AWOKE WHEN he should not have done so, and freed himself from the blanket and half rolled, so that his hand fell onto the knife at his belt. A night bird called somewhere to the east and a woodland creature snuffled in the undergrowth, but it was not those which had woken him. He took a moment to read the few stars visible through the branches and the ropes of cloud, and saw that a little of the night remained. He did not believe danger to be close, but he gripped the handle of the knife, and called on its power and it flowed into him and roused him fully, and sharpened his senses. He scanned the length of the small valley, steep sided, rock strewn, tree filled, for what had disturbed him.

There was someone to his north, in the blackness a little below the ridge, moving softly between the trees. He called on more power from the knife until he could see the shape, still now, half crouched behind a trunk.

The figure took a step and straightened and paused, tall and slender, well balanced. A woman, a girl, he decided, at the exact moment that she spoke.

"I saw you pass after dusk. The moon was setting and I believed you would be unlikely to go on. Here would have been my choice to camp. I thought to check on you." Her voice was young, and light, and may even have held amusement. She stepped away from the tree, perhaps to present herself. She was cloaked to the ground, with a wide hood thrown back. He would have liked to see her face, read her expression, but would draw no more from the knife. Should he deplete it, it could take half the morning to replenish, and he may have need of its power before then.

She did not approach – though whether for her own safety, or to save him from apprehension, he did not know.

He sat and reached for his boots. The wrappings on his feet had loosened, and he took time to position them and to fasten his boots with care. "You are alone. Is it safe to be so?"

"You are no threat to me in my woods," she said.

"I do not wish to be." He put away his knife. "*Your* woods? Do you possess them or inhabit them?"

"I bide here for a while." She moved down then, graceful and confident, to stand on the edge of the small clearing. She held a staff, shoulder high, which he had not perceived before, and he wondered about that.

He stood. "I have ham and oatcakes, and would offer you hot dandelion to drink, if you consider a fire acceptable in your woods."

"If you are not hiding. I believe you are avoiding attention. If so, you have chosen well. The curve of the valley and the height of the ridge will hide any flame. And I assume you have the skill to make a fire without smoke. I shall accept your offer of breakfast." She leaned the staff against a tree and sat with her back to a rock and her knees under her chin. She covered her head with the hood, and appeared to go to sleep.

He scraped a flatness with his boot and lit a small fire, and used the light from it to collect wood more suitable for heating his cooking pot. He clambered the two score paces down to the river for water, and stood there for a while, listening to the night. The dry summer had much reduced the river and he strode across it and looked back. The ridge above his fire showed its line of trees against a sky paling with approaching dawn.

She was kneeling by the fire when he returned. Her face turned up to him for a moment, and her eyes and cheeks caught the glow. She looked down before speaking. "Few come this way. The others passed in the dark, two nights ago. They carried torches, and made a deal of noise. They did not fear discovery. Do you seek them? Or do you avoid them? I do not think you are one of them. I did not like them and I did not challenge them."

"For now, I follow them. They are dangerous. They have a stolen item. I am charged with its recovery." He used a stick to pile embers and shape the fire to fit his pot. He blew into the redness and the light grew and the flames curled and he watched as if the resolution to his difficulties could be found therein. "Two nights ago. Then I am not gaining on them."

They shared the meal and talked of the weather, the dry early summer, and the abundance or otherwise of the various plants in the woods. She told him of the small river, the Went it was called, largely unrecognised, but with a significance in the region.

She finished her drink and stood and said goodbye, collecting her staff and vanishing into the shadows. He sat for a while. At full daylight he removed traces of his fire and shouldered his pack and set off north. The hills were gentle, the morning fine and the walking pleasant. He sensed many ancient paths and ways here, overlaid with modern roads, meeting a few miles ahead of him, a town of some size and some antiquity. This would be a market town.

The signs he was following were a mile or so to the west – those he pursued avoiding the town, he guessed. He himself would pass through the town and replenish his pack at the market. He would find the trail again somewhere to the north. The old ways were covered and lost among buildings and gardens and he took the roadside pavements, the roads now filling with traffic. He passed signs of quarrying, sandstone and limestone, abandoned and neglected. This was a town with stone strong in its past.

There was a castle, ruined, a small distance ahead, which he felt strongly though could not see, and a river passing through towns to the north and to the east. Its waters would not meet those of the Went for many miles.

He found a small park planted with shrubs and flowers, and with curving paths, and took that to remove himself from the traffic for a short while, then climbed a series of flights of steps along a very ancient way, and crossed a busy road. A little higher still, he could see a church tower, a clock face set in darkened stone, and he went towards it and reached a market at the centre of the town.

The market was active, pleasant in the morning sunshine, and by it was a structure whose existence he had been aware of for a good while. It was a rectangular construction of arches, perhaps a dozen paces across, stone, old, with something more ancient beneath it. Many of the old ways and lines and long hidden paths met here, and the lady of the woods was sitting on the steps waiting for him. In good light she was only a little older than he'd thought, and she wore the uniform of a nurse.

She tilted her head at him and smiled. "My other life," she said, at his silent appraisal of her. "Do *you* have one?" She tapped the step by her side with her fingertips as an invitation, and he sat.

"I build and repair roofs," he said, "when I need to." He watched the market and the folk. "I haven't needed to for a while."

"We have a good roof above us," she told him. "It was built to shelter the young ladies who sold butter and cream and cheese, part of the market. Other goods were sold here." She smiled at this, but said no more.

They watched without speaking the flows of the buyers and the activities of the traders, behaviour unchanged for centuries, beneath the superficiality of the different clothes and goods.

"Your quest." she said. "It is more difficult than you wanted me to believe."

"I have to remain on foot. I would lose the trail otherwise. They do not have to do so. Though they have done mainly. They will stop somewhere and I will reach them."

"You believe them to be dangerous?"

"They should not be to me. I will find them and take back what I seek."

She turned and faced him. "I have been in contact

with our principals. This is an important quest. Worthwhile. But you need help and I should join you. My craft can support your skills."

He breathed in to speak, but did not do so.

"It is what we do. I know of no others in the area available." She stood. "Wait for me. Two hours. Less. I have matters to attend to. Equipment to collect. I shall return here."

"Your other life?"

"I can withdraw from it without difficulty."

She strode away down the hill. He stood and looked around and chose a direction. Amongst the trivial, this was a good market. Bread, cheese, meat and fruit; he would fill his pack and return to these steps and sit and wait.

The town itself intrigued him. He would visit again once his task was completed.

But north first, and with a companion.

# Princess Annabel's Birthday Party

*Ann Rhodes*

*Artist: Dianne Ibbertson*

IT WAS A DARK NIGHT in Pontefract. The moon and stars had been kidnapped by Princess Annabel. "Much easier for me to be out and about without them buggers watching," she told the owl who tapped on her window to complain about the darkness, "I won't be long….."

She blew out all the candles in her bedroom and slid down the twisting bannisters, told the king's wolfhounds to be quiet, threw her blue cloak around her shoulders and crept outside the castle. She moved very fast, over the drawbridge, past All Saints Church, up the hill into the Valley Gardens to where the witch lived in a cave at the bottom of the cliff.

Tonight she was going to sort out that witch once and for all. She was fed up to the back teeth of her spells causing trouble everywhere and there was no way Princess Annabel was going to let the witch spoil her 18th birthday party, the grand ball the King and Queen had planned for next Saturday night at their castle in Pontefract.

The witch had just returned from her book club and was making supper so she was not pleased to see Annabel heading her way, but she was too late to cast a barring spell. "What do you want?" she growled, stirring her pot furiously.

"Social call," Annabel said, wondering what was in the pot because it smelt really good.

"Brought my invitation to your birthday party, I suppose?" the witch growled and Annabel shook her head.

"In your dreams!" she said and moved closer to the fire, "'I've just come in to warm up because it's very cold out there tonight."

Now Annabel knew a bit of magic too, and in the castle garden she had carefully gathered the herbs for her spell and wrapped them in an oak leaf. All she had to do was scatter them in the fire and the witch would not be able to leave her cave until well after the party.

The witch shrugged and turned back to her bubbling

pot. "Be my guest," she said, "but don't be long, I am expecting company. And company you won't like…"

Annabel stretched her hands to the fire and dropped the herbs into the flames.

"Ohh if you want to be like that, I am off!" And she left with a huffy swing of her cloak.

Outside the cave, she tossed the oak leaf to the wind. But, because it was so dark, she did not notice that the leaf had curled up at the edge and a tiny sliver of her herb potion had not gone into the witch's fire.

Annabel went back to bed and forgot all about the captive moon and stars until the owl tapped on her window to complain again; and when she leaned out of her turret window to release them, she thought she heard the witch cackling.

The days before the Grand Ball were very busy. The fairy musicians were refusing to play because they claimed they hadn't yet been paid for playing at the New Year Party. And if they were not playing their fairy fiddles, the Snow Queen and Winter Lord would not attend. And if *they* did not attend, no-one else would! Annabel alternately stamped her feet and cried as she saw her haul of birthday gifts diminishing with the possible lack of guests.

And then Annabel found that her beautiful emerald silk gown was too long, so the seamstresses went into a flurry of needle-threading and stitching.

"Mind them spindles," Annabel warned, "I am not as daft as Princess Aurora. I am not falling for that one at *my* party!"

Everyone was so busy that they did not notice that the witch had not been seen for a few days. Everyone except Annabel, that is. But some nights as she blew out her candles, she thought she had heard the witch's whisper crackling through the night air.

Annabel did not realise that her spell had failed

because the witch's visitors had found the curled leaf outside the cave and the witch used the remaining herbs it contained to banish the spell.

On the evening of the party, the sun stayed shining up in the sky later than usual so he could see the fine carriages driving up to the castle. This upset the moon and stars who were already fed up with Annabel for kidnapping them. So that when the witch asked them to help her with a little joke at Annabel's expense, they gladly agreed.

All she asked them to do was to draw a cloudy veil across the midnight sky so that she could slip into the castle unseen.

Once they had counted their back pay, the fairy fiddlers had agreed to play and soon glittering carriages and magic carpets were arriving at the castle, ball gowns rustled, diamonds shone and feet began to tap to the music.

Annabel didn't need her mirror to tell her she looked stunning in her emerald dress and sparkling diamonds. But the mirror told her anyway because the last time he had forgotten to praise her, Annabel had thrown a shoe at him and it had hurt.

The King and Queen greeted guests and Annabel curtsied, demurely swept her lace fan through the air and gracefully accepted the many gifts they brought. Soon the gold table under the chandelier was groaning with parcels of every size and shape, all tied up with beautiful ribbons. Annabel longed to rip open the lovely wrappings. But her mother, the Queen, had warned her to behave like a lady for the evening; and, for once, she did as she was told. Instead she danced prettily with all the young men who clamoured to partner her.

Just after midnight, the King clapped his hands and called for a chorus of Happy Birthday as Annabel prepared to cut her birthday cake. The Queen handed her a shining silver knife and, as the last notes of the birthday song faded away,

Annabel turned and  raised the knife to cut the first slice of the lovely pink-frosted cake.

It was at that very same moment that the witch, having crept unseen right up to the door of the ballroom, blew her black crystals into air, aiming them straight towards Annabel.

The crystals, deflected by the shining knife, settled – not on Annabel, but on the shoulders of the King and Queen who both promptly lay down on the polished dance floor and slept, snoring loudly.

The witch had already made her escape by then but Annabel heard her laughing, "Happy Birthday, my pretty princess, you shall sleep for a hundred years no matter who tries to kiss you!"

There was pandemonium in the ballroom.  Guests pinched themselves to make sure they were awake, carriages were called for, the apothecary was dragged from his bed and servants were summoned to carry the King and Queen up the winding stairway to their bedroom on the top floor of the castle.

The apothecary declared that the spell was a strong one and must take its course of one hundred years.  The fairy musicians were refusing to leave without payment and the King's favourite wolfhound was halfway through the cake.

Annabel tucked the King and Queen into their enormous four poster bed, slid down the bannisters and threw everyone out of the ballroom – although she did first pay the fairy musicians, as she knew exactly what tricks they were capable of playing.

When the great room was empty, she kicked off her dancing slippers and somersaulted the whole way around the room.

"I am the king of the castle!" she sang, "And you're a dirty rascal!"

The witch's sigh flickered through the candlelight.

38

Annabel turned her attention to the golden table overflowing with boxes; with wild abandon she ripped each one open, throwing the pretty ribbons, bows and glittering wrappings about the floor, thrilled with each beautiful birthday gift uncovered.

She shared her cake with the wolfhound, sitting amidst the strewn wrappings, and decided that she would make the most of the hundred years before her parents woke up.

In her cave, the witch was hastily packing up. "No way are we staying here with that young hussy in charge," she told her cat, "we'll come back in a hundred years."

In the ballroom Annabel grinned.

"Goodbye! And good riddance!" she cried and the witch's sigh grew fainter and fainter.

Annabel blew out all the candles and went off to sleep in the best guest bedroom, the room she was never allowed to disturb. And she let the wolfhound sleep on the bed, splashing the lovely pale blue lace quilt with the icing and cream he was too full to lick from his paws.

# The Museum Rocking Horse

*Susan McCartney*

**Artist: Brian Lewis**

"THIS IS DEAD BORING. Why are you dragging me in here?" The boy Liam  kicked the cast iron mangle with some force.

"Pack it in, Liam," Rosie turned and looked up at him. "You're supposed to be in College and it's not like I dragged you kicking and screaming into the museum.  You decided to tag along.  I'm the one who's supposed to be researching for an essay."

He muttered something which Rosie didn't catch.

Sometimes he wondered why he liked her so much. She wasn't his usual type – the tall leggy blonde.  Rosie was tiny with dark hair, cropped short like a pixie.  Her clothes were something else – as if she had rummaged through her Granma's wardrobe looking for jackets and dresses and found the most moth-eaten and old-fashioned. Her eyes though were the darkest blue and made him weak at the knees.

"Seeing that you fudged your GCSEs, you should be doing your Maths right now. In class, remember! At College, remember!'

"Fudged? What do you mean?" He scowled.  His handsome face creased into a frown.

"I'll spell it out for you. F.U.D.G.E.  Your GCSE results. You failed the lot. Remember?"

"We're doing Algebra and all that 'x' business is a load of rubbish. Pointless.  Who needs it?  Anyway, Dad's bound to give me a job in his office."

"I can show you," she said.  "Once you get the knack, it's a doddle.  Just think of 'x' being a fluffy pink cloud. Who's scared of fluffy pink clouds?"

Liam looked at her as if she'd gone mad and, with a curl of his lips, went to kick a metal Dolly Tub.  Rosie grabbed his arm, pulling him away.

"Look at this display of Liquorice.  I love it – especially the old packaging.  My Nan's Mam used to make Pontefract Cakes.  Mam says they went to visit when she was

41

a little girl and took a box for her Gran but the old lady wouldn't touch them, couldn't stand the smell." She laughed. "Ate too many when she was on the production line."

He looked unimpressed. "Can't stand the stuff. Let's go to mine and play *Call of Duty*. It's dead good – loads of shoot-ups and body parts."

"Great Gran used to make munitions as well. I'm going to write it all up for my Assignment."

"Your Great Gran made bombs?" Surprised, he looked down at her.

"That interested you and that's something," said Rosie. "Real people and not made-up stuff with cyborgs and robots and people getting shot to bits."

"Yeah," he said. "Bet you think you're so clever just because you passed all your exams."

Bristling, Rosie turned to him, hands on her hips.

"I'm no genius. Take the Maths, I had to work really hard before it clicked. Tell you what though, I'm gonna succeed and get a decent job. And under my own steam."

"I bet you get loads of help," he whined, shoving his hands in his pockets. "I hate Maths and I'm the only one in the class that knows nada."

"So the big brave special forces soldier is scared of a fluffy pink cloud that calls itself 'x'".

"Am not," he muttered.

"Got your College stuff with you?" she demanded, refusing to look away. He shuffled his feet, thinking that it had been a bad idea to go to the museum.

"Yeah. And... ?"

"Right then! I'll show you some short cuts if you want." Frowning, she studied him for a moment. "Did you have any dinner? You look dead pale. With that black shirt and jeans you could pass for a stick of liquorice yourself – one with a toilet brush for hair that is!" she added under her breath.

She laughed as he grunted, unimpressed. "Mum's going get me the latest *Halo* for Christmas plus tons of other stuff. It would be dead neat to be a soldier in those days."

Rosie knew *Halo* was a shooter video game. Now it was her turn to grunt. Then she sighed with a weary roll of the eyes. "I'll show you something you might like." She hauled him through the glass doors to the English Civil War section.

"And you call this entertainment? It's pathetic!" he scoffed.

"You can be such a shit sometimes, Liam."

Indifferent, he stared at the exhibits, scowling at the soldiers dressed in their plain old ordinary coats and with trousers to the knees. When he saw the children's pale rocking horse sitting in the corner of the room, he snorted in disgust. The horse stood, its ears thrust forwards and its nose facing downwards. Coarse black hair hung down one side of its head and over its right shoulder, a brown leather saddle astride its back.

"Like anyone is going to believe they were riding in the cavalry on that thing!" he jeered, "It's kid's stuff!" Liam waved a dismissive hand at the model soldiers. "Where are the weapons and all the battle gear? Look – they're not even tooled up. One of them is wearing a woolly hat. What use is that? Some soldiers!"

Irritated, Rosie snapped back: "This is *real* history. I just thought you might have been interested."

He turned to the rocking horse and the box of dressing-up hats. A sly grin twisted his lips. "I'm gonna have a go on that rocking horse. Pass me that floppy hat with the feather. Better still, hand me the one from the model."

Hands on hips, she glared up at him.

"Can you not read the notice? This is for the kiddies to play on. Not a big numpty like you. You'll have us chucked out."

Liam sneered. "So what? This is all rubbish – dead feeble. Give me *Halo* over this waste of space. Imagine being a soldier of the future and taking out the trash. I'd be invincible. I'd be a hero."

"No. Wait," she said.

Ignoring her, he reached for the horse. His fingers touched the reins when dizziness swept over him in a sickening rush. A swirling black chasm reached up to grab him.

*Where was he? The ground felt hard and lumpy. Face down, his nose was full of grass and earth. What had happened? Something hard and heavy thudded into the ground inches from his head. A horse's hoof. This was impossible. All around him lights flashed and fires raged. Fragments of metal and stones hit the ground, sending up clouds of dust and debris that stung and tore into his skin. Clapping his hands over his ears, he tried to deaden the sounds without success.*

*Boom! He was under attack. He could hear the screams of men and horses, the clash of steel on steel. He screamed, turning away, desperate to block out the carnage. All about him he saw the dead and wounded and smelled that odour that he knew was blood. This was no re-enactment, no video game – the battle was real and he was in the middle of it. Defenceless with no battle armour or laser gun and no Special Forces soldiers to rescue him.*

*"On your feet, lad," a harsh voice commanded. A drum was thrust into his hands. The man wore only a suede coat, hat and those funny trousers for armour. These were already blood-splattered. His only weapon was an ancient musket. "Our Officer is gone and you'll have to do. Sound the signals when I tell you."*

*Liam stumbled to his feet and tried to speak but words wouldn't come. Tears dripped down his chin along with snot and the blood from the cuts on his face.*

*This had to be a nightmare but he couldn't wake. Smoke filled his nose, eyes and lungs and his chest screamed for air. The smell of gunpowder, acrid and biting, was everywhere, attacking the eyes, making them stream. Musket balls, stones, nails, and bits of metal bombarded them. It was a rag bag of an army. Some men carried muskets and others long poles. A few had breast plates and helmets, though these offered little protection from the enemy – whoever they were.*

*Then he saw them. At full gallop, men on horses charged towards them, their gleaming swords held at shoulder level. Like a rabbit caught in headlights, he stood transfixed. He was going to die. One of the horsemen had a dog sitting on his saddle. If he had not been so frightened, he would have laughed at the sheer craziness of this. Swords flashed and men fell, wounded, dying. He was caught in the middle of hand-to-hand fighting. There was no time to think – he tried to lift a fallen sword but staggered with the weight of it.*

*As swords flashed about him, he knew he couldn't stand it for a moment longer – the men who were bundles of bloody rags, the screams, the pungent smells, the choking smoke, the debris pebble-dashing his body. A sword blade pierced his shoulder. Sounds in his ears roared like a windstorm. Liam screamed, his stomach heaved and he was sick. A patch, warm and wet, trickled down from his groin.*

He fell to his knees sobbing. "Mam, Mam, help me! I don't want to die!" His voice a pleading crescendo.

Again his world whirled; the vortex that had caught him now spat him out. The next thing he knew, Rosie had grasped his arm.

"Get a grip, Liam. We're in a public place. You'll get the curator coming over." Rosie rolled her eyes, not sure whether she was worried or annoyed.

He stared at her. "What the …! What happened? Where am I?"

Rosie gripped his shoulders and stared into his eyes.

"You sure you're alright? You gave me a right fright."

He managed a weak nod.

"One minute you're trying to get on the rocking horse, then your eyes kind of fluttered. Next thing you're shouting the place down."

Liam shivered and straightened himself up. He was alive and back in the safety of Pontefract Museum. He rubbed a shaky hand over his face, over his shoulder. But there was no blood, no wounds, no wetness. He was in one piece. Relief swept over him like a warm bath. "Sorry," he said, leaning his head against cool wall tiles. "Just felt a bit dizzy."

"That's your own stupid fault for not eating enough. Let's get out of here and grab a sandwich."

"A chip butty?"

She gave him a quick kiss on the cheek and shook her head. "A ham salad sandwich would be better," she said, "if you are not allergic to vitamins?"

Liam gave her a wobbly smile. "You think you're so funny." He sagged; the stuffing had been knocked out of him.

"Let's get that grub," she said.

Relieved to be leaving the Museum, Liam turned round to have a last look at the rocking horse standing so innocent in the corner. It seemed to him that the rocking horse was laughing. Its lips curled back showing large yellow teeth. He gawped and the horse gave him a cheeky wink. He closed his eyes and counted to three but when he opened them, the horse winked at him again, its long lashes closing over dark eyes. A whinny echoed through the Museum.

Liam choked back a scream. "Rosie – did you see that?"

But she hadn't. For she was already outside and he was speaking to a swinging door.

# James Edward Smith

*Walter Storey*

*Artist: Jane Walsh*

*BORN: 24$^{TH}$ AUGUST 1896   Died 27$^{th}$ September 1916.*

Uncle Arthur was sat next to David, my brother. Arthur and my brother had a special relationship. Arthur had been married to my mother's sister, Grace. When Grace died, Arthur and Grace had been married for over 60 years. Most large families had an 'Uncle Arthur and Aunty Grace' in those days.

Arthur and Grace had had no children of their own but had a special place with their nieces and nephews. David had a special place with Arthur, and Arthur had a special place with David. Now they were sitting together on the sofa, finishing a bottle of whisky that had somehow survived since Christmas. Arthur was 90; and he started telling us about his oldest brother, Ted. Ted was totally new to us; we knew Arthur had had several brothers and a sister, but we had never heard of Ted.

Apparently Ted had been his oldest brother and had been killed in the First World War. The story Arthur told was that when the War started, Ted was just 18, old enough to join up and wanting to join up for the 'great adventure' but he was not allowed to join because he worked down the pit. The country needed coal as much as it needed soldiers.

In 1916 the army was running out of men, so they sent round to the pits and asked if they could spare any men. Each pit manager decided how many men could go without affecting coal production. The manager of the pit where Ted worked calculated how many men he could spare.When it was decided how many men could go and join the army, the brass tallies – those things with each work number that the men handed in before they went down the pit – were put into a flat cap. They shook the tallies up and, if your number was picked, out you could go. Ted's tally didn't come out, but his mate's did.

Now Ted's mate had just got married and there was a

baby. Ted swapped his tally with his mate, and off he went.

Over 450 men between the ages of 18 and 45 from Pontefract had died in the First World War. We decided to find out all we could about Ted.

At first it was very difficult. We had been told that he died in the Battle of the Somme. We checked various web sites and found that at least 350 Edward (Ted) Smiths had died in the first day of the Battle of the Somme. Then we had some luck. (Is that the right word?) A friend with more computer skills that we had found his name listed in the local evening paper, with the address of his mother, Arthur's mother. It was Ted! His full name was James Edward Smith. He had died in September 1916, from wounds he received in the Second Battle of the Somme.

From these bare facts, and the census, we tried to tell Ted's story. Ted was born in Pontefract. It appears that his mother, Mary Jane, had relatives in Tanshelf.

We think she moved to these relatives for her confinement. She had five children who grew to adulthood. Ted was the oldest, then there was Arthur, twin boys George and Tommy, then a girl Maretta. At her christening, apparently, the vicar had had too much sherry, and what was supposed to be Mary Etta, came out as *Maretta*, so for the rest of her life she was Maretta.

Their father William worked 'down the pit' and all his sons eventually followed him. The family moved around the Yorkshire coal field, eventually ending up in Hunslet, South Leeds, and working in the Middleton Pit.

When Ted Smith was wounded, his legs had to be amputated and he was moved to a military hospital outside Boulogne where he contracted gangrene. In 1916 his mother was told he 'had died from his wounds'. He is buried in a cemetery that was attached to a military hospital at Terlincthun on the outskirts of Boulogne. In 2014, with descendants of Ted's family, I visited the cemetery. We were the first of his family to visit. His mother could not afford to go to France.

The Terlincthun British Cemetery is vast; it contains 4,378 graves from the First and Second World Wars: including some Germans and some civilians who were caught up in the wars. It is a well-cared for place, beautiful in its awfulness. And still used. Frequently the bodies of soldiers are found on the former battle fields. Attempts are made to find out who they are, uniform buttons and other metal badges being clues, and they are then respectfully re-interred in this cemetery, their graves marked with the details that are known.

We stood in silence. It was the silence of respect, but it was also a silence to remember Ted and the journey a Yorkshire lad had made to this foreign field.

Ted joined up in 1916. The first wave of the war had happened. Historians argue that 1916 was the most difficult year of a bloody and difficult war. He must have known that the 'great adventure that would be over by Christmas' was a fallacy. There had been Christmases with families mourning their dead brothers, sons, husbands and fathers. The long casualty lists were published and the casualties who survived were coming home. He must have known that if you joined up, you stood a good chance of being killed or maimed. Soon. He still joined up. He swapped his disc with his mate and went off to war. He died. Not a quick glorious death, but a slow painful death, without his legs, forgotten except by his brother who many years later told his story.

It's 100 years since Ted Smith joined up. His generation were told that they were fighting a war to end all wars – yet in that hundred years there has been only one year, 1967, when Britain was not at war. Those of us around in 1967 remember Northern Ireland, but apparently that does not count.

What did Ted die for?

# Mrs T and the Buffaloes

*Brian Lewis*

*Artist: Charles Windsor*

PONTEFRACT COUNCIL has a long history of making unusual decisions. In the 17th century, following the third siege of the Castle by Parliamentary troops, Mayor Hill petitioned Westminster to knock down the Palace/Castle and in that way return the citizenry to the tranquillity which had been a feature of Good Queen Bess's reign.

The petition was heeded. Pomfret Castle was torn down and the town was robbed of a majestic building which, if it was standing today, would be equal to Windsor Castle.

The stone, glass, lead and timbers were then sold off to the building contractors who made up the Council. The Mayor's coat of arms bore a legend in Latin; in English it would have read "It's an ill wind that does nobody any good".

I have often wondered if the 17th century Mayor Hill was any relation of a Mr Hill who told the fledgeling 'official Labour candidate' in the 2012 election that he would show her his arse if she won. Spurred on by this incentive, she brought in three times as many votes as the opposition!

Pontefract is distinctive where buildings and politics are concerned. In the 18th century, the Buttercross was given to the town by Solomon Dupier, the man honoured as the traitor who ceded Gibraltar to the English during the War of the Spanish Succession and who came to live in Pontefract after receiving a pension from the British government. And the Town Hall rose on the remains of the town walls after they came down. Left in place, the walls would have rivalled York – but, as the intellectuals in the Civic Society agreed: "What went up when other things came down created next year's history".

It was in a downstairs room of the Town Hall that the Castleford heroine Viv Nicholson often went to be married in a room that became the local Registry Office in the 1970s. Viv boasted that, having won £152,000 – several millions in today's money – she would 'spend, spend, spend', and she did so. She went from dire poverty to extensive riches and back again in less than five years. A distinctive house in Garforth celebrated her good fortune. In the great scheme of things, this was a minor feature on Yorkshire's architectural landscape compared with changes which occurred in the room that overlooked Pontefract's market place in the mid-19th century.

The most impressive feature of the Town Hall – a space mentioned in Professor Pevsner's *Architectural History of England* and called the Nelson Room – occurred then. In what was once the town's courtroom, today at the far end is a plaster bas relief of one of the panels from the base of the column in Trafalgar Square, London.

The way it reached the town was odd. It was offered to Mayor George Green in 1855. He hired a horse and cart and moved it north. He thought that the relief was a gift; the sculptor Carew, on the other hand, thought that he had sold Pontefract Council a valuable art work. The Aldermen and Councillors said nothing; instead, they adopted a wait-and-then-wait-a-little-longer policy. After a couple of decades, the sculptor got something but not a lot.

The subject was an odd choice of architectural decoration. The nearest seaside point was Robin Hood's Bay, 60 miles away, and Nelson was long dead. The relief showed the admiral's last moments and over the top was the signal that the famous admiral sent out to the fleet as the ships of the line moved forward to confront the French. It read *England Expects Every Man To Do His Duty.*

In 1984 during the Great Coal Strike, these words overlooked the heating cabinets from which the Prince of Wales Colliery Miners' Wives Support Group doled out beans on toast to members of the National Union of Miners and their families. It was also these words which led the Council to endorse an invitation from a Pontefract 'friendly society' to Prime Minister Margaret Thatcher to come North and unveil a commemorative plaque.

Downing Street was surprised by the invitation to

visit Pontefract but in the interests 'one nation Conservatism', her private secretary decided to pass it on. The hand-written letter read:

*Madam, On the authorisation of the Grand Primo of the Royal Antediluvian Order of Buffaloes (Turks Head, Pontefract) I would like you to unveil a 'blue plaque' in our Town Hall.*

It was a strange yet innocent invitation, and that is possibly why it was passed around Number Ten and eventually came to rest in the in-tray of the researcher Griselda Sidcup. In a pencilled pedantic note she observed: "This organisation is barking mad. It has no authorisation for *Royal*, this was a printer's error. It should read *Loyal*. Since it was founded in 1822, it cannot be *antediluvian* since this means before Noah's Flood. That said, since, unlike the Freemasons, it is open to public scrutiny, it is no threat to the State".

There was no recommendation. But, because it was a distraction from the main political issues of the day – global warming, the loss of the nation's manufacturing base, 'evil empire' USSR and the cost of remaining in Europe – the Head of the Civil Service passed it on to the PM, for it would be useful to have a decision, any decision, on that particular Monday morning.

Mrs T, as she was affectionately known by her staff, liked making decisions but she did not like the researcher who had triggered it. Too pretty by half and educated at Cheltenham Ladies College! So she scrawled across the bottom of the letter. "Ignore the advice and then sack this girl. Both my beloved father, a Grantham grocer, and my husband Dennis, are Antediluvian Buffaloes. I find this young woman's remarks insensitive. I will go to Yorkshire." The word *will* was underscored three times.

She had complicated reasons for going North. Her decision to wreck the NUM had not been taken lightly and at times she had thought that the government would not succeed in the task. She might have defeated Argentina and sunk the Belgrano, but flying pickets and battles like the one at Orgreave were in a different league. In England she could not countenance a single death, for support for her aggressive policy was not universal. On the other hand, in her own words, she must not show that she was 'frit'.

The previous year had been a hard year because the class demarcation lines by and large had collapsed. In Northern towns like Pontefract even Conservatives had supported the soup kitchens and saw that when Arthur Scargill's miners' union went under, so did the brass bands, choirs that sang the Messiah, and possibly the Great Yorkshire Show.

No-one respected her or her Government in the industrial North, what husband Dennis called her "nether regions". She needed to go back into areas like Pontefract and re-establish her authority. She felt that a market town amongst coalfield villages was the sort of place where she might succeed. For goodness' sake, it had a ruined castle and traffic lights, though not – as she was ready to admit – the essence of civilisation: a cathedral and Betty's.

Originally she had thought that she might give the hospice a couple of mechanised beds rather than stand in front of a plaque and speak in platitudes, but her spin doctor felt that overt exposure to the dying was potentially troublesome. He said: "It would be a disaster to be cursed with her last breath by a toothless crone. Best keep it simple, Margaret. There is little can happen at a blue plaque occasion".

Yorkshire had a sort of Wild West attraction for her. She had never fully understood why the women and men of the Ridings hated her so fervently, for the essence of Conservative thinking could be found in the Yorkshire Man's Motto:

*See all, hear all, say nowt.*

*Eat all, sup all, pay nowt.*
*And if thou does owt for nowt*
*Do it for the sen.*

Some say that it was the strike-breaking practice of putting soldiers into Metropolitan Police uniform that was overtly confrontational and caused the dislike. A Rotherham man on trial for GBH and breaking a scab's fingers said: "It was not the action of kicking the shit out of us that was upsetting but the lies. I hate deception."

Mrs Thatcher had stayed at Chatsworth overnight and – to make thing simple and avoid crowds – arrived incognito without publicity dressed in Dame Edna Everidge spectacles at one of the town's three stations. So she was surprised to find a welcoming committee.

The anonymity had been deliberate. "It is too soon after the Strike to do much", her enforcer had informed her as she left London. "Arrive in Pontefract, get a taxi, MI6 will see to that, be greeted by Geoffrey Lofthouse MP, go upstairs at the Town Hall, have your photograph taken looking into Market Place, go over to the plaque, pull the cord, show an interest for 90 seconds maximum, say *Thank you*, go out through the back door and get into our car and move off, move off *immediately*. You can have a comfort break at Lord St Oswald's home."

What she did not realise was that the people who met her at Baghill Station were not real Buffaloes but typical local Labour Party members in disguise. Everyone had played in a Rugby League Final at Wembley, so they were professionals at forming an impromptu line and shaking hands. This Rugby experience was an important qualification if you were to be a Labour candidate in any of the five towns of Wakefield. The real Buffalo Brethren were paid not to come.

As the train came to a halt, the sham Buffaloes formed a sort of Morris Dance formation. The performance

56

was a bit ragged. But, as she stepped onto the platform, Pontefract's Member of Parliament, the perfectly suited Sir Geoffrey Lofthouse, himself an ex-miner, walked towards her and welcomed her with: "Margaret, how good to see you here in my constituency."

She liked men who were not afraid of her. Real men, generals and the like. "Geoffrey. How lovely to see you too!"

"Unfortunately," said Sir Geoffrey, "I did not know you were coming. I came out without shaving as soon as they phoned me to give me the details of your visit. My friend here will look after you. I have to go to a funeral."

This was a lie, he was off to Tescos, but no-one challenged the excuse of going to 'a funeral'. Like the phrase 'ladies' problems', it was never questioned. "It is no-one close, an old comrade." With that, Sir Geoffrey kissed her on both cheeks and was gone.

The unnamed friend spoke. "It seems daft to get a taxi when the Town Hall is just beyond yon Flats." With that, *She Who Was Usually Obeyed*, regretting her high heels, followed by an insipid man in a beret smoking a pipe, whom she assumed to be MI6, and seven incognito Councillors dressed in the formal gear of the Royal Antediluvian Order Of Buffaloes, formed an impromptu single-file procession and walked silently towards John Poulson's Horsefair Flats.

At the junction where the Station Drive met Southgate, the leader stepped into the road and raised his hand. The traffic stopped. A car window went down and a young lad leaned out.

"Who is the woman?" asked the driver's wife.

"You know, she used to work with yer Mom stamping handcrafted Deluxe Liquorice Cakes at Dunhills. She lived up on Chequerfield in the house downside of Fred the Poltergeist's house."

They did not go onto Horsefair but went towards the Town Hall's back door and turned immediately left and then left again and entered through the double door. On the way up, she discarded the spectacles and, when asked by a Buffalo's wife if Her Ladyship wanted to powder her nose, simply said: "Pardon me?"

Hearing this, and thinking it was a code, the Secret Service man took his Sherlock Holmes pipe out of his mouth, stuck the stem in his ear and said: "Roger, Roger, are you hearing me?" into the bowl.

Some things are too daft to laugh at so the Prime Minister entered the main room at speed, irritable, anxious to get away as quickly as possible without a lot of fuss.

The Nelson Room contained an assortment of respectable local people who were in the know: Civic Society, Lions' wives, English Heritage folk, subscribers to the *Readers' Digest* and the *London Review of Books*, Round Table people – but not Quakers and other subversives. The Chair of Governors of a local school shook her hand and ushered her to a Chippendale chair on loan for the occasion from Nostell Priory but did not comment on that fact. He knew that a gentleman would not mention expensive furnishings, though a more plebeian Labourite might.

The Chair of Governors said it was an honour to have on the same podium three children who came from aspiring working class origins and who went to Oxford. He mentioned their colleges, though paused before he said Mrs Thatcher's College – Somerville. He was unsure if women were being given degrees when the Prime Minister went there. For her part, Mrs Thatcher, the wife of a millionaire, was never sure of how she should play the feminist or the class-origin card and so did not respond. Sleeping with a rich divorcé was less than relevant in the story of her ever-upwards progress.

Then it was the turn of a much-loved local scholar/historian, who had no such misgivings. He got down to detail immediately. He said: "We're here today to remember the strikes and battles which have given Britain the courage to initiate a welfare state and to dedicate ourselves to its maintenance." After a pause, he went on: "We need to know that there is an alternative history to the history of kings and such things. The author whom we are honouring today, as the Second World War moves into history, wrote a masterly book called *The Common People*. Here, as the words above the bas relief of *The Death of Horatio Nelson* imply, England expects ever woman and man to do their duty. The man we are honouring in our own way expected us to honour the wealth that we have in common."

With that, the MA Oxon invited the Prime Minister to pull on the velvet cord and reveal the town's newest Blue Plaque. She had no alternative but to do what was asked. In silence she read to herself:

*I became a Socialist because as soon as the case for a society of equals, set free from the twin evils of riches and poverty, mastership and subjection, was put to me, I knew that to be the only kind of society that could be consistent with human decency and fellowship and that in no other society could I have the right to be content.*

There was no way out. But then, as pedants will, she saw a mistake. The author's name was spelt incorrectly. She turned and faced the audience, hitting the plaque as she did so.

"He was a Balliol man, his name was GDH Cole – not," she paused, "not GDH Dole. Cole not Dole. Cole not Dole."

# Liquorice Faire

*Linda Jones*

**Artist: Dianne Ibbertson**

MARIE STEPPED OUT of the car and breathed in the sweet aromas of summer. Above her head a branch of a cherry tree hung low; the dappled shade was very welcome. Paul turned with a smile, a wisp of dark hair rising gently on the summer breeze. At his feet, leaves skittered and raced, caught up in a sudden gust of wind. It tugged at Paul's sleeve, the white cotton stark against sunburnt skin. A drum beat, low and insistent, began and Marie shivered as a song echoed around the car park.

> *Full was the blossom upon the tree.*
> *Where first her gaze fell upon her true love*
> *A garland of pink to crown her fair beauty*
> *They danced to the beat of the drum*
> *Hey, ho and merry fa la dee*
> *They danced to the beat of the drum.*

A group of excited children ran out from behind a van. Clad in fairytales, they were laughing and singing, determined to dance their way to the Faire. Distracted, Marie smiled, following their journey. And like a breath, the song faded, leaving only the briefest of memories.

Patiently Paul stood in line for a ticket. All the while he watched her as she waited under the cherry tree. She was so beautiful. Idly he followed the slim lines, the sweep of her neck. Hair gilded bright as the midday sun. The hem of her forget-me-not blue summer dress floating easily about her ankles. She was his sea of calm. He sighed, still hardly daring to believe that she could love him... A drum beat – a song, faint at first – began again. He turned, trying to work out where it was coming from.

> *And sweet was the cherry upon the tree*
> *Where first he kissed the lips of his true love*

*A garland of green to adorn her fine hair*
*They danced to the beat of the drum*
*Hey, ho and merry fa la dee*
*They danced to the beat of the drum.*

Shrugging, he turned back. She was running slender fingers over the bark of the tree. An icy chill gripped his chest and for a moment he could hardly breathe...

Marie was tracing the outline of a heart, cut deeply into the trunk. Inside, roughly hewn was M & P...? Thrilled, she was instantly caught up in a whirl of imagined lovers and trysts... when something soft and red landed at her feet. And immediately the drums began again.

*And red was the berry upon the tree.*
*Where first she swore never to be parted*
*A garland of leaves to adorn her bright mantle*
*They danced to the beat of the drum*
*Hey, ho and a merry fa la dee*
*They danced to the beat of the drum*

With a shiver, she stepped away, out into the sunlight. There had to be a song contest or something going on. Whatever it was, she wished they'd change the tune.

"Do you like my costume, Mister?" A knight, no more than thigh high, cloaked and booted, ran up to grin at Paul.

"I certainly do." Paul shook off the strange sensation and smiled. This had to be his mystery singer.

"I'm going to enter the competition," the knight declared stoutly, "Do you think I'll win?"

"If I were a judge, for definite," Paul declared. "And I'd hire you as my minstrel, so you could sing for me all the time..."

"Me? Sing?" the boy scoffed, "I can't sing for toffee."

"Then you'll have to be my knight protector instead, especially with the helmet and that sword you're carrying."

With a sweep, the wooden blade flew from the scabbard and the knight grinned. "Cool. Now I'm a knight on a quest. Gotta go, I'm off to find the rides..."

Ticket for the car sorted, Paul held out his hand.

"I'm surprised there are still so many cherries left," she said, glancing up at the laden branches.

"And they are as red as your lips," he stretched to touch the swinging berries. "But I doubt they would taste as sweet."

"So you heard that weird singing as well," she laughed, slipping her hand into his. "I was beginning to think it was just me. There's Dave and Sarah. Let's catch them up."

Under their feet the grey of concrete soon gave way to the uneven cobbles. Jostling bodies, clad in rainbow-coloured garments, ebbed and flowed around the bustling stalls. Cajoling cries rang out, eager to attract a willing crowd. The Liquorice Faire was in full swing.

"Just fifty pence a ride!"

"Get your punnet of strawberries, two for a pound."

"Finest quality Italian leather; belts, handbags....!"

"A rose for your lady, sir!" A wrinkled hand thrust the palest yellow bud toward him. "Only a silver coin..."

Paul gazed into dark pools that looked up from her ancient face. The drums began again as all other sound faded away.

> *And rough was the bark upon the tree*
> *When first he cut deep their names together.*
> *A ring he vowed to place upon her finger*
> *They danced to the beat of the drum*
> *Hey, ho and merry fa la dee.*
> *They danced to the beat of the drum.*

"For your true love," the old woman whispered, "A rose picked at dawn will keep her safe..."

He looked down and in his palm was a fifty pence piece, silver bright. He felt heat as she plucked the coin from his fingers and relief as he pinned the bud to Marie's breast. A moment later he was back, blinking in the bright sunlight.

"Wow! Did you hear that?" he looked about, trying to work out where the old woman and the singer had gone. But with a playful laugh, Marie pulled him away, tender fingers stroking the delicate flower.

In the afternoon heat they walked hand in hand along Salters Row to Market Place. Tasting olives and cheeses, they feasted on roast pork, fine ales, liquorice and sweetmeats. They sat under canopies to hear folk songs and tall tales; talked with friends, laughing, enjoying... Yet time and again, Paul shifted uncomfortably, looking over his shoulder, trying to work out where the drums and the whispered song were coming from.

*And few were the cherries upon the tree*
*When first the Weaver spied her fine beauty*
*A garland of thorns to set upon her fair hair*
*They would dance to the beat of his drum*
*Hey, ho and merry fa la dee.*
*They would dance to the beat of his drum*

"Did you hear that?" Paul asked, turning to Dave, "That song about the cherries?" But Dave merely shook his head and offered him another pie.

Again they strolled among the stalls, admiring glass-blown tree and whittled owl.

"A gift for such a beautiful woman?" Sharp eyed, high booted, the stall holder smiled all too kindly at Paul. But as the man draped a scarf about her head, in a cloud of softest blues and pinks, Marie shivered at his touch.

"It *is* pretty," Paul said, unaware of her unease.

"For such beauty I charge only a small silver coin. Here, let me fasten it for you."

She couldn't move. Her legs, arms had invisible cords wrapped tight about them.

Again a silver coin gleamed in his palm, and the world began to spin. Paul stared down at his hand, unable to move.

The man's breath was icy cold. Like sand it scraped across her cheek, bone-thin fingers dipping to her chest. But a hiss, serpent-like, escaped from his lips and he leapt back, as blood, just a single drop, sprang from his finger.

"Not for me," she said, the words sounding distant and strange... With an effort she sent the scarf fluttering to the bench.

An old woman stepped to her side, ancient eyes sharp, brooding.

"She has made her choice." And with a firm hand she closed Paul's stiff fingers over the coin.

Instantly his world and hers came back into focus. Marie looked about, wondering where the old woman had gone.

"I think I've had too much sun," she murmured.

"That makes two of us. Maybe we should invest in a hat?" Laughing, he kissed her lightly and drew her away.

They rode on a rattling shuttle-bus to the remains of Pontefract castle, where careless children ran helter-skelter down and up the grassy mounds. Ranged left and right were colourful stalls, with their pennants flying high. The owners, clothed in medieval garb brewed and stitched, whittled and baked, while all about them the old stones held on to their secrets, silent, brooding...

"Well, I'll be damned! It can't be..." The surprised cry stopped them in their tracks. They turned to find a woman, clothed in linen apron and dress, staring at Marie as if she'd seen a ghost. "Only you're the spitting image... Frank! Come and take a look!"

A portly man stepped out from the side of the stall and did a double take.

"My God!" he declared. "Why, it's like we've gone back 25 year. Same hair... even to the colour of dress."

Unsettled, Marie moved closer to Paul,

"I don't understand," she said, looking between the baffled couple.

"Sorry love," the woman smiled hesitantly, "It's someone we met here at the Faire, see... only she disappeared."

"Aye, her and the lad she were with," the man added. "Police hunted for weeks after..."

"Well, I wasn't born 25 years ago..." said Marie.

"Aye, well, it's just one of those things." The woman's broad face smiled out. "Why don't you choose sommat nice from stall? Half price, especially for you."

Paul bought Marie a ribbon, wide banded, with simple daisies sewn all along and another of palest blue.

"Let me," he said, loving the way her hair rippled softly between his fingers as he tied in the daisies.

They stood in the shadow of the ruined gatehouse listening to the tales of the castle and all the while Marie tried not to think of the lost girl...

"Do people see lots of ghosts around the castle?" a young voice demanded, as the leather-clad enactor paused to wet his ailing throat.

"Aye, well, there are a few stories right enough. Especially about hangings, of course. Mind, back then they'd hang you for just about anything. Stealing a loaf of bread as like as not... There's one tale about a grave in the grounds of All Saints Church, where they do say every year a bunch of pure white lilies appear, regular as clockwork...'

Beside her, Paul shivered.

"Are you cold?" she asked, though the sun was still warm on her back.

"Just someone walking over my grave," he laughed and turned bright eyes to smile down at her. "How about we walk back and find somewhere to eat?"

Marie was busy talking to one of their friends when the gleam of silver caught his eye. A ring? He bent to the grassy bank and scooped it up. It shimmered in the late afternoon sun. A small blue stone sparkled up at him, only glass but the colour was so like her eyes. It made him smile. He looked closer. There were no markings. It was hardly more than a child's fancy but he slipped it into his pocket...

"Sarah said there's some good music on tonight about nine," Marie suggested, as they began to walk back toward Micklegate. "It's outside, near the Buttercross..."

"If you're up for it, so am I," and he raised her hand to kiss the soft skin.

Back in the town, they sat with a group of friends for a while, eating and drinking, enjoying the day as it slipped into evening. A cacophony of sound began to build, spilling out onto the streets. The bar they were in was soon crowded, the benches packed, the noise rising as the ale flowed.

"I'm off to try and buy us a drink," Paul said, leaning in so his lips touched her cheek. "I might be some time."

Beer glasses scattered on the wooden table were a living sculpture of amber and cream. Caught up in the moving shards of light, it was hard to make out the echoing drums and song.

*And black were the berries upon the tree*
*When darkness fell, her love lay a-dying*
*A garland of lilies to lay upon his grave*
*She danced to the beat of the drum*
*Hey ho and merry fa la dee*

*She danced to the beat of the drum.*

"Who is that?" she demanded of no-one in particular. The woman next to her looked at her strangely, before turning back to her friends with a shrug.

Her searching eyes found him at last. Paul was standing not far away, talking to a friend. The drinks he had bought sat on the ledge beside him. Relieved, she relaxed, not quite knowing why she was so tense. But an icy fear gripped her as the stranger's hand hovered over the two glasses... Something fizzed, sending tiny bubbles cascading up through both drinks.

More people hurried into the already crowded room. Panicking, she began to push her way through, only to see Paul was already moving toward her.

"Sorry to be so long. Only Dave was asking if we wanted to go over to his next weekend." He raised the glass to his lips ready to sip,

"Don't!" she pleaded and leant into his side, whispering frantically. "Let's just go home," she finished, desperate to get as far away as they could.

"Why would anyone spike our drinks?" he murmured. But she was already halfway to the door.

Outside, the air felt heavy, without a hint of a breeze, and still she shivered. She tried not to keep looking back, but the hair on her neck prickled with every step.

Sensing her fear, Paul gripped her hand more tightly.

"Not far," he promised as they turned into the car park. But as the words left his lips, a fierce wind gusted, blowing leaves and dust high into the air. Marie dropped his hand, coughing and spluttering, trying to wipe the debris from her eyes.

"Paul!" cold bone fingers were groping at her ankles, a mist was rising.

Her scream tore through him like a knife. Why

couldn't he see her? The wind – the dust was everywhere!

"Marie! Keep talking! Keep yelling!"

"I'm here!" she pleaded, "Stretch out your arm..."

The heat from his touch shot up her arm. He grasped her fingers, her hand, pulling her to him.

"I've got you, just hang on..."

They battled their way across tarmac, through a wind that screamed insanely, dragging at arms and legs, biting and tearing with teeth of stone and wood. Through it all the drums and the song echoed around and around

*Gone were the leaves upon the tree*
*When first they cut the bitter earth to lay her*
*No other man will taste her fair beauty*
*She'll not dance to the beat of the drum*
*Hey, ho and a merry fa la dee*
*She'll not dance to the beat of the drum.*

They were at the cherry tree, its branches creaking and groaning. Only a few yards away the car stood, though it might as well have been a mile. They couldn't move.

"Grab the trunk!" yelled Paul.

She clung on; icy mist pooled at her feet and all the while bone-thin fingers clawed up at her.

He was leaning in, desperate to keep her safe. Something small and sharp jabbed hard into his thigh. He moved. But again, like a penknife, the small ring dug in, refusing to be ignored.

"Marry me," he blurted, the words muted in the screaming wind.

Marie blinked up into his dark eyes, not quite believing what she'd heard.

"I love you so much!" he cried, defying the wind. "I can't imagine life without you! Please, Marie, say you'll marry me!" Pulling out the silver ring, he gripped her hand

and slipped to his knee. Murderous voices raged, tearing at hair and clothes but he clung on.

"I will," she cried.

The ring slipped so easily onto her finger... Instantly the wind died as if it had never been. Above their heads, the tree stilled, the night became clear and calm.

As the car finally drove away, the old woman regarded the Weaver with an air of defiance.

"You lost." The words were flat, cool. She turned and with a flick of her head began to walk. With each step, the years fell away.

"*This* time!" he growled in acknowledgement. "But more will come, though none will ever be as fair as you, my sweet Mary."

Turning, she regarded him with startling blue eyes, long gilded tresses shimmering under the moonlit sky. At her breast she held a bunch of pure white lilies.

"And you will never have me. I would die at my own hand a thousand times more." And with the forget-me-not blue of her dress floating about her, she disappeared into the shadows of the night.

# If Only They'd Known

## *Robin Gledhill*

**Artist: Babs Smith**

"HE NEVER DID!" said Reg.

"He did!" said Fred.

"He never!"

"He did!"

"In that case," said Reg, "I'll get the beers in." He went off.

"Who's *he*?" asked Tony

"Joe," said Fred.

"What about him?"

"He did…"

"He did what?"

"He passed."

"I'm going to hit you in a minute! Joe did what?"

"Passed his exams."

"Oh well! That calls for a celebration. Where is he anyway?"

"On his way. He just called. That's how I knew." Fred Johnson looked at his life-long pal Tony Everett and smiled. They had grown up together; and now, both 22 and single "but still looking" as they put it, workmates and neighbours, they shared a common interest in beer and women.

Their other life-long friend Reg Laner – who was now at the bar getting the drinks in – and Joe Southern, had all been to the same schools and colleges and now the same firm of printers. Joe was a year older than the other three, had been taken on as an apprentice earlier, and therefore qualified first.

Reg came back from the empty bar with three pints of bitter. "He never did!" he said.

"Don't start that again," said Tony.

Reg grinned. "Only joking, mate. Has he told you about Joe?" He nodded towards Fred.

"Eventually," said Tony, "and I reckon when Joe turns up, we should have a bit of a celebration, tomorrow being Sunday and all."

Fred's phone beeped. "He'll be here in five."

"I'll get him a pint," said Reg, walking back to the bar.

"Game of pool while we wait?" said Tony.

"Sure. It won't take long anyway."

"In your dreams, Hurricane!" Tony set the balls up. "Just for that, you can break."

"Hi guys!" came a shout from the Red Lion doorway as Joe bounded in, grinning from ear to ear.

"Who's a clever boy, then?" Tony said, leaning on his cue, waiting for Fred to take his shot.

"Me, me and me!" said Joe. "Where's Reg then?"

"Getting your pint, my Lord," said Fred, lining up another shot.

"See you in a sec then." And Joe went to the bar.

"Come on Fred, hurry up. I'm growing a beard waiting for you."

"Go bollocks. You're watching skill at work here."

"I'm watching paint dry, you mean."

"Sod it! Now you've made me miss. Two to you."

"Thought you said you were good at this. What did you used to play – Pot White?"

"Just take your shots, you sarcastic pillock."

"Right, lads," said Joe  as he and Reg returned. "I propose a pub crawl. Not literally. However, if we end up on hands and knees, so be it."

"Okay, one in here, on to the Liquorice, across to the Elephant, up to the one by Smiths and then along tot' Tap. All agreed?"

"All agreed!"

"Told you you couldn't play," said Tony as he potted the black, picked up his pint and proceeded to finish it in one. "Liquorice it is and it's my round."

That said, the lads shouted their goodbyes and headed next door to the Liquorice Bush.

They were single, twenties, manual workers, all learning the printing trade at Pontefract Press. Concerning girlfriends, they had all been partnered up at some time or another, but decided that Saturdays was always lads' night out.

The four played for Ponte Union. That said, Tony and Reg had been approached to trial for Castleford Tigers. Both were waiting on the results.

Tony was six five in his socks, eighteen stone, and fit due to weekly weight training. Dress sense tended to be governed by his size, in that most of his clothes were of a sports nature: fleece or club blazer, jogging bottoms and sweat shirt. If he occasionally looked like a sack of spuds, no-one was about to tell him.

He strode up to the bar, passed pleasantries with the young barmaid and ordered four bitters, pointing to a pump. He winked at her when she brought the beers over. "Cheers, love. I'm Tony," he said.

"I'm Amy," she said, "Ten pounds forty, please."

"Have one yourself, Amy." Tony handed her a twenty note.

"Cheers. I'll have a lager. Thanks." Amy poured herself a pint of Carling and rang the money through the till. "Your other half wouldn't be impressed," she said as she brought his change back.

"I don't have one," he said.

"Neither do I."

Tony took out a pen and paper and wrote his number down. "I'm at a lonesome moment tomorrow night if you fancy doing anything."

Amy wrote on the paper, tore it in half, handing her number back. "Call me."

Tony walked back to the lads. He looked like the Cheshire cat with a limp.

"Did you make those yourself?" said Fred, "Only

we're dying of thirst over here."

"Just sorting out tomorrow night."

"Jesus Christ! You don't hang about, do you?"

"Now we've *all* got to pull for tomorrow night," said Reg.

"Challenge accepted!" shouted Joe.

Amy looked across at the lads and smiled.

"Right, guys, the Elephant awaits. Onwards and sideways. Come on, arses in gear!" said Tony. On his way out, he looked at Amy, blew a kiss.

She smiled, signalled *I see you*, turned to carry on serving a customer.

*Little did she know.*

Cheerful and happy, joking and upbeat, still sober, they crossed the market square to the Elephant. They wandered down the alleyway.

"Tony, tha's a brass-necked bugger," said Fred.

"Still can't believe you asked her out for tomorrow," said Joe.

"Well, when you've got it… !"

They entered the pub and sauntered up to the bar.

Fred ordered the beer. "How about a round of shots?"

"Right on!" said Joe, "Now you're talking. Party time!"

"Sit down and I'll bring them over," said Fred, noticing a pretty girl serving behind the bar. The others went to a table and sat down.

"We're celebrating our mate's educational prowess," said Fred to the young lady after he'd ordered the beer and four Sourz, "Would you like a drink?"

"Cheers," she said, "A Vodka Red Bull. They're on offer this week."

"I'm Fred."

"I'm Mandy, and don't say can you fly me. Although

*nearer the ground* is a definite maybe."

Fred smiled, took out a piece of paper and a pen and wrote his number down. "How about coming out tomorrow night?"

Mandy wrote her number on the piece of paper, tore it in half and handed hers back to Fred. "Call me."

It was Fred's turn to be a limping Cheshire cat as he took the tray of drinks back to the table. Tony took one look at him. "You sly dog! You have, haven't you?"

"Two-nil," said Fred

Reg said: "Down to us to keep the team up."

"Easy," said Joe, "The Borough will be a cinch. Let's try for a two in one."

"Sounds a bit rude," said Tony.

"I meant two girls in one pub, you arse."

"Shots at the ready," said Fred, "One, two three down." With that, four Sourz vanished.

The pints quickly disappeared.

"I can understand Tony," said Reg, "but you... !"

"Thanks. You're no Adonis yourself. I do my bit for Darwin and the species."

Now Fred, who worked out the same as the rest, but was much shorter at five nine and twelve stone, was nonetheless a fine rugby player. Unlike Tony, Fred was able to wear style.

He wore a smart charcoal grey double breasted suit, light red shirt and quality paddock black boots.

Reg favoured the sports image. He took to leisure shoes, jeans and polo shirts with a team fleece. He stood six two and sixteen stone. A rock in the Forwards, as his friends often said.

"Come on, you lot. The Borough awaits Joe and me!" said Reg, "You know. Birds waiting and all."

"Christ, you're common!" said Fred.

"Desperate situations call for such measures, my

friend," said Reg.

"All right, let's get these two connected," said Tony.

They downed their beers, said their farewells. Fred blew a kiss to Mandy and smiled. She signalled *I see you*, smiled, turned to carry on serving a customer.

*Little did she know.*

"Whose round is it?" said Joe.

"You know damn well, cheapskate. Just because we're celebrating *you*, doesn't mean you have to have short arms and deep pockets for the night," Fred said.

"All right, only having a laugh! Four, and how about Sambucas?"

"Quality," said Tony, "Bring it on."

"Right, Reg, you and me to the bar," said Joe, "We're on a mission."

"Fiver says you shit out!" said Tony, as the two walked to the bar.

The Borough was expected to get busier, so the landlord had laid on extra staff.

Unfortunately for Joe and Reg, there was only one girl behind the bar. Undeterred, Joe caught the girl's eye and she came over. "Four bitters and four Sambucas please. I'm celebrating passing exams."

She came back with the drinks. "Clever dicky, aren't we?"

"Would you join us in a drink?"

"Only if my friend can have one as well."

"Where is …?"

"*She* is in the loo. She won't be a minute."

"Two Malibu and cokes, if you don't mind. My name is Joe and this is Reg."

"Pleased to meet you. I'm Sandy and – here she is. Denny. She *hates* being called Denise. Here, Denny, these nice young men have just bought us a drink."

"Cheers, guys. You can buy us one tomorrow if you're in town."

"Are you working in here again?"

"No, silly. It's our night off and we plan to enjoy it."

Joe looked at Reg and winked. "Pen and paper, please, Reg." Joe wrote both names and numbers on the piece of paper and handed it to Sandy. She looked at Denny, looked at the lads, looked back at Denny and smiled. Denny wrote her number and handed it to Reg, whilst Sandy gave hers to Joe.

"Tomorrow it is then," said Reg.

"Call us," said Denny.

Joe and Reg walked back to the table where the other two were sitting.

"You have, haven't you?" said Tony, grinning as he handed Joe a fiver.

"We have, haven't we?" said Joe, looking at Reg. "Four nil. Sunday here we come."

"And again, one, two three down!" said Joe.

The Sambucas disappeared, closely followed by the pints.

"And now the Tap and Barrel," said Joe.

They bade their farewells to the two girls, waved and left in a line. The last two out were Joe and Reg, who blew kisses.

The girls both signalled *I see you*, smiled and turned to carry on serving customers, Denny to the left, Sandy to the right.

*Little did they know.*

As they walked out into the square, all four shivered. The temperature had mysteriously dropped to what felt like freezing in the space of 20 minutes. This was bizarre for mid-summer. Joe hadn't dressed for a cold spell. He was wearing trainers, jeans and a sweat shirt. Standing six dead and 14 stone, he was normally able to cope with cool. "Brass monkeys!" he said, "I'm freezing my knackers here."

"You're a soft tit," said Fred.

"It would be a good idea to leg it to the Tap," Tony said, "I reckon we should kitty up now."

"Good idea, but be quick. They're dropping off!"

"Tenner each?" said Tony, "That way there's more shots."

"Good call," said Joe, "only please be quick. I'm losing all feeling somewhere."

They handed their money to Tony.

"Onward, men!" he said.

As they turned to walk to the Tap , they realised they couldn't see a thing. They'd been intent on sorting out the kitty, and a dense mist had descended on them.

"This way!" said Tony, taking the lead, the others following very closely behind. Through the mist they saw the welcoming lights of a pub.

"Here we are!" said Tony, "Told you I'd find it."

"It looks a bit different," said Fred, "I don't remember that sign." The pub sign seemed to glow.

"Probably new," saidTony. "After all, we haven't been in here for at least five weeks."

"True," said Fred as he followed Tony into the pub.

It seemed unusually busy compared to the others in town. Tony ordered. "Four bitters, four Tequilas and four Sourz, please."

"Sure thing," said the man behind the bar, "I'm Ted. Celebrating?"

"Joe here has just passed his exams. Fancy a drink yourself?" said Fred.

"Cheers, I'll have a lager if I may."

"No probs, mate."

Ted's name badge said *Terry*. He brought the drinks

back. "Thirty notes please, including mine. And congratulations."

"Thanks," answered Joe.

Tony handed over a twenty and a ten. They turned to look for somewhere to sit.

"Busy night? said Tony.

"Twenty-first of June," said Ted or Terry, "the big one!" He moved off to serve another customer.

The lads looked at each other, shook their heads in unison and headed off to the one remaining table in a corner booth. At least they had a good view of the stage.

"And again, one, two three down!" said Tony and the Tequilas, salt and limes were gone.

"Once more! One, two three down!" This time the Sourz were gone.

The DeeJay sidled up to the booth, switched the system on and began to play a very strange style of electronic sound. The pub crowd were really getting into this sound except for the lads who were beginning to feel a little odd. They looked across at the barman and smiled. He signalled *I see you,* turned to carry on serving the customers.

*He knew!*

Back at their table, the four were out of it. Staring blankly across at each other while the music became more intense. A low chanting came from the crowded pub as the customers slowly congregated round the stage. Only the lads remained seated.

From the back of the stage emerged a hooded figure in black. He was followed by 12 similarly dressed men. Eight of them walked over to the lads and picked them up and carried them to the stage. The lads seemed paralysed and did not resist. The hooded leader walked up to each in turn as they stood rigid on the stage. He placed a hand on their foreheads, each in turn, muttering something about the summer solstice.

Sunday morning was a warm start to any day. Tony woke up and rubbed his head. He looked around and saw familiar surroundings and was very puzzled. Then he heard a voice in his head. It was Fred! Fred and Joe and Reg! They had all woken at the same time with the same strange feeling. Whatever had happened was going to change their lives forever. They had become telepathic.

They all knew. And later they said they knew. And later, the girls would say so as well.

This was going to be an interesting year.

Fiction from Nettle Books

# Heaven Scent
John Winter
*A comic novel set in the swinging sixties.* Charlie wanted to be part of the sexual revolution but it sort of passed him by. But he and fellow reporters on a seaside weekly paper have something to take their minds off summers of love – when the sleepy resort is rocked by mystery explosions. Is it the Isle of Wight Republican Army?
**ISBN: 978-0-9561513-6-0**                    **£10**

# Homer's ODC
Michael Yates
*A darkly comic novel of terrible murder and even more terrible poetry.* When gangster's son Raymond is shot in the head at a Yorkshire bus station and falls into the arms of wannabe poet and user-of-the-mental-health-services Barry, all hell breaks loose. And the balance of power is changed forever in the world of organised crime.

**ISBN: 978-0-9561513-7-7**                    **£10**

www.ingramcontent.com/pod-product-compliance
Lightning Source LLC
Chambersburg PA
CBHW071418170626
46811CB00003B/1450